WHEN THE Wizzy Foot GOES WALKING...

BY RONI SCHOTTER

ILLUSTRATED BY
MIKE WOHNOUTKA

DUTTON CHILDREN'S BOOKS

For Lena Rose Reibstein and for Mark and Lauren,
her wonderful Wizzy Pop and Wizzy Mum
—R.S.

For Cayden, Cora, Cohen, and my
own Wizzy Foot, Franklin
—M.W.

DUTTON CHILDREN'S BOOKS
A division of Penguin Young Readers Group

Published by the Penguin Group

Penguin Group (USA) Inc., 375 Hudson Street, New York, New York 10014, U.S.A. • Penguin Group (Canada), 90 Eglinton Avenue East, Suite 700, Toronto, Ontario, Canada M4P 2Y3 (a division of Pearson Penguin Canada Inc.) • Penguin Books Ltd, 80 Strand, London WC2R 0RL, England • Penguin Ireland, 25 St Stephen's Green, Dublin 2, Ireland (a division of Penguin Books Ltd) • Penguin Group (Australia), 250 Camberwell Road, Camberwell, Victoria 3124, Australia (a division of Pearson Australia Group Pty Ltd) • Penguin Books India Pvt Ltd, 11 Community Centre, Panchsheel Park, New Delhi–110 017, India • Penguin Group (NZ), Cnr Airborne and Rosedale Roads, Albany, Auckland 1310, New Zealand (a division of Pearson New Zealand Ltd) • Penguin Books (South Africa) (Pty) Ltd, 24 Sturdee Avenue, Rosebank, Johannesburg 2196, South Africa • Penguin Books Ltd, Registered Offices: 80 Strand, London WC2R 0RL, England

CIP Data is available.

Published in the United States by Dutton Children's Books,
a division of Penguin Young Readers Group
345 Hudson Street, New York, New York 10014
www.penguin.com/youngreaders

Designed by Jason Henry
Manufactured in China • First Edition
ISBN 978-0-525-47791-4
1 3 5 7 9 10 8 6 4 2

Shhhh!!
Can you hear it?
Listen! It's coming....

Early every morning, the **WIZZY FOOT** rises
From its sleep, in the deep, undercover.
Wriggling and twitching its itching **WIZZY** toes,

It makes ready to hunt all the creatures it knows.
When the **WIZZY FOOT** goes walking,
Stalking...
There's *no* mistake—
Floors shake, buildings quake,

The cat,

the dog,

a sister wake.
Meow. Woof! Stretch. Yawn.
"Leave us *alone!* It's barely dawn."

"Fee. Fi. Fo. *No!*" it replies.
Then, with a *terrible* grunt,

The WIZZY FOOT lures them off on the hunt.
"Fee. Fi. Fo. Fum."
It spies...

In bed...the WIZZY MUM!
Then, "Who's *THAT*?" it cries.
(What sharp eyes!) Nearby her lies
The WIZZY POP!

It clumps, then stumps, right on their bed!
It bumps them, jumps them, calls for bread
(or toast with strawberry jam!).

It's morning and the hungry WIZZY FOOT is itching
To have munchings and crunchings in the kitchen.
"Throw open the cabinets!" it commands.
A WIZZY FOOT *needs* to eat
Bowls and stacks of Wizzy Treat!
SOON it is filled with Wizzy power
…Watch out!!!

Its tummy stuffed now with eggs and buns,
It runs,
Then stomps and whoops it up.
It taps and bangs, and will not stop.
Eeny meeny miny moe.
It simply will *NOT* tiptoe!

If anyone is working,
It's *lurking*....
It doesn't like to be left alone.

It *hates* when someone's on the phone.
Is that the sound of crashing toys?
Of course! Don't you know?
It *loves* noise!

But if someone dares to scold it . . .
If *"QUIET INSIDE!"* a WIZZY MUM's told it,
Then—Huff. Puff. *Stamp*. Boom.
An *angry* WIZZY FOOT leaves the room.

It howls. It hisses! It hoots and cries.
It puts on boots and runs outside

To splash in puddles and stomp about,
Daring someone to follow it out.

Race it, chase it, try to snatch it?
The WIZZY POP will have to catch it.

Keep it in his arms a while,
Try some tricks to make it smile.
Hold it close to stop its wiggles,
Tickle it until it giggles. 'Cause…

A happy WIZZY FOOT is a glorious thing!
It skips and hops and tries a two-step.
It twists and shouts and dares a new step.
Hot-to-trot and hip-to-dip, it's awesome—cool!
A WIZZY FOOT, happy, is a Dancing Fool!

Yes, all the way through till the end of the day,
A WIZZY FOOT's busy—forever at play.

It wants a story.

It needs a song.

It drifts off to sleep,
But not for long....

Just when all's silent and safe,
One would think,
BUMP! THUMP! STAMP! TRAMP!
The WIZZY FOOT goes walking...
In search of a drink.
"What's all that noise?"
"Is there a riot?"
"Will there *ever* be quiet???"

What more, indeed, can a WIZZY FOOT need?
The WIZZY POP to hug it, the WIZZY MUM to snug it.
No wrestling, just nestling—one cozy last kiss,